THE FORGETFUL BEARS MEET MR. MEMORY

by LARRY WEINBERG

illustrated by BRUCE DEGEN

SCHOLASTIC
HARDCOVER

SCHOLASTIC INC. / New York

To Jane and Heather and Michael and Lara—
and to Sam behind the scenes.
—L.W.

For Chris,
Who puts up with a
Very Forgetful Bear.
—B.D.

ISBN 0-590-40781-3

Text copyright © 1987 by Larry Weinberg
Illustrations copyright © 1987 by Bruce Degen
All rights reserved. Published by Scholastic Inc.
SCHOLASTIC HARDCOVER is a trademark of Scholastic Inc.
Art direction by Diana Hrisinko. Text design by Sarah McElwain.

12 11 10 9 8 7 6 5 4 3 2 1   7 8 9/8 0 1 2/9

Printed in the U.S.A.   24

First Scholastic printing, January 1987

ONE MORNING, all the alarm clocks in the Forgetful house went off at once. "Why are we getting up so early?" they asked each other. But no one remembered.

"Look!" cried Roger. Hanging from the living room ceiling was a big sign that said:

DON'T FORGET YOUR TRIP!

Grandpa Forgetful scratched his head. "Trip? What trip?"
"Why don't we get ready for one?" suggested Mrs. Forgetful. "Then maybe we'll remember it as we go along. Let's hurry so we won't be late."

They all dressed quickly and ran to the front door, where
they found another sign. It read:

GO BACK! YOU FORGOT YOUR BAGS!

"Oh, I remember now!" said Mr. Forgetful proudly. "I left them in the closet." But then he forgot which way to go and went straight out into the backyard.

When Mr. Forgetful saw the garbage cans outside, he scratched his head. "Now, what was it I came here for? Didn't someone say bags?"

He pulled two garbage bags out of the cans and hurried off to the car to join the others. Everyone was waiting for him as he jumped in.

"Where are we going?" Phoebe asked.

"That," said Grandpa, starting the engine, "is a very good question." But he forgot to answer it.

Just then, they heard someone shouting from behind. Roger looked back. "It's our neighbor. He's running after us!"

"The poor man must need some help," said Grandpa, slowing to a stop. "What can we do for you?" he asked politely.

Gasping and panting, the neighbor caught up to them. *"You can give me my car."*

"Oops! Sorry!" cried the Forgetfuls.

And back to their street they went.

"Our own car is a much prettier color, anyway," said Mrs. Forgetful as they drove off once again.

"But we *still* don't know where we're going!" cried Phoebe.

"Yes we do!" Roger pointed to a sign on the windshield that said:

YOU FORGOT YOUR TICKETS TO HAWAII!

"No I didn't!" grinned Mr. Forgetful. "Now I remember everything. I remember that I made these signs myself! And I remember that yesterday I packed the bags — and put the tickets inside!"

"I'm so proud of you!" exclaimed Mrs. Forgetful. But when she looked in the bags she found nothing but garbage. "You took the wrong bags!"

"Sorry, dear," he mumbled. "But a fellow can't be expected to remember everything, you know."

Grandpa turned the car around, and back they went to the house.

This time Mr. Forgetful went to the closet and pulled out the right bags.

Mrs. Forgetful did the driving and found the airport without getting lost. Roger found out exactly where to find the plane that was leaving for Hawaii. And Phoebe, rushing up the runway, shouted, "Hold the plane! My daddy has the tickets!"

The flight attendant looked at the ones in Mr. Forgetful's hand and shook his head. "I'm afraid, sir, that these tickets are for a basketball game."

"Well…well, maybe they are for a game in Hawaii," said Roger hopefully.

"You'll need the right tickets," the flight attendant said. "But you still have a little time to find them. We don't leave until noon."

Once more the Forgetfuls climbed into the car. "I'm getting so tired of going back and forth and back and forth!" cried Mrs. Forgetful. "Why can't we ever learn to remember things?"

"Well, this time it's going to be different!" vowed Grandpa. "This time we really mean business. Right, everybody?"

"Right!"

As soon as the Forgetfuls got home they searched everywhere for the missing tickets.

"Mommy, here is the wedding ring you lost!" cried Phoebe.

"Phoebe, here is the birthday present you meant to give me," said Grandpa.

"Grandpa! Here is the tree you brought home last Christmas," called Roger.

"Roger, here is your — no, it's *my* wallet!" shouted Mr. Forgetful.

"Quick!" the others all yelled together. "See if the tickets are in there!"

Mr. Forgetful turned his wallet inside out, but he couldn't find the airplane tickets.

"I can't stand this anymore," he said.

"Neither can we!" And all the Forgetfuls sat down to be sad together.

Just then, there was a knock on the door. Mrs. Forgetful dried her eyes and answered it. There stood an old elephant in a battered hat.

"Excuse me, ma'am," he said. "I observed from the mailbox
outside that your name is Forgetful. That's very interesting,
because my name is Memory. And helping folks remember
is what I do for a living."

"Come right in!" they all shouted.

"Why, thank you very much. Do you think there's something
I can help you with? I don't charge very much at all. I'm willing
to work for peanuts."

"We need to find some plane tickets to Hawaii right away!"

"Aha!" said Mr. Memory. "Then let's get right to work. Now, I want you all to stand in the middle of the room and sway from side to side like elephants."

The bears got up and began to sway like elephants.

"Very good," said Mr. Memory. "Now I want you all to lift your trunks up over your heads the way I'm doing."

"But you *have* a trunk," said Roger. "We only have noses."

"No problem," smiled Mr. Memory, opening up a bag he was carrying. "Put these hoses on your noses."

"But those," said Phoebe, "are from vacuum cleaners."

"That's true. But growing a trunk would take too long. So put one end on your nose and hold the other up in the air."

"I really don't see how this is going to help us remember at all," mumbled Mrs. Forgetful.

Mr. Memory stared at her. "Have you found a *better* way?"

All the Forgetfuls lifted their noses.

"Perfect!" said Mr. Memory. "And here comes the most important part of all. I want you to say after me, 'Now I am an elephant. And an elephant never forgets!'"

"Now I am an elephant," repeated all the bears. "And an elephant never forgets!"

"Say it again and again until you believe it."

"But I don't *want* to be an elephant!" Phoebe whispered to her brother.

"Do you want to go to Hawaii?"

"Now I am an elephant," said Phoebe. "And an elephant never forgets. Now I am an elephant…."

"I'm starving," said Grandpa, after a while. "Are there any peanuts in the house?"

"Excellent!" said Mr. Memory. "All right, elephants. Start remembering. Who saw the tickets last?"

"What tickets?" asked Mr. Forgetful.

"The ones you need for your trip," said Mr. Memory.

"What trip?" asked Mrs. Forgetful.

"To Hawaii!" said Mr. Memory.

"What's a Hawaii?" asked Grandpa.

"I can't believe it," said Mr. Memory. "You've become the Forgetful Elephants!"

"What's an elephant?" asked Roger.

"Oh my, oh my. This is terrible!" moaned Mr. Memory. "I've become too old for this work. I'm no good anymore. I'll never be able to help anyone again!" He plunked down on the sofa and began to sob.

Mr. Forgetful whispered in his wife's ear. "We really must do something for the poor fellow."

"I could give him some tea and cookies," she replied softly. "That's always nice when someone is unhappy. But I can't remember where I put the cookie tin."

"I believe…" sniffled the elephant, "…I believe that I may be sitting on it." He stood up and sighed as he gave the tin to Mr. Forgetful. "I'm afraid I made a mess of *this,* too!"

"No, it's all right," said Mr. Forgetful gently, as he straightened out the can. Suddenly, his eyes grew wide. "Look, everyone!" he cried. "Here are the tickets! I must have put them in here so I wouldn't forget them!"

"I'm very glad for you," said Mr. Memory in a tiny voice. "But this is *not* the way I wanted to help you find them."

"Oh boy!" cried Roger, glancing at the clock. "It's already past noon. We missed the plane!"

"The one that leaves today, perhaps," said Mr. Memory, glancing at the tickets. "But those tickets are for tomorrow."

"*Tomorrow! Tomorrow! Tomorrow!*" shouted the Forgetfuls. They hugged Mr. Memory and they hugged each other. They danced and sang and had a party. And the old elephant felt much better.

The next day, Mr. Memory took the Forgetfuls to the airport
and saw them off. The Forgetfuls flew all the way to Hawaii
and had a wonderful time — which they never forgot!

E
WEI
    Weinberg, Larry
       The Forgetful Bears
    meet Mr. Memory

	DATE DUE		